Atheneum Books for Young Readers
An imprint of Simon & Schuster Children's Publishing Division
1230 Avenue of the Americas
New York, New York 10020

The illustrations for this book are rendered in watercolor, colored
pencils, and gouache.

First Edition
Printed in Hong Kong
10   9   8   7   6   5   4   3   2   1

Library of Congress Cataloging-in-Publication Data
Priceman, Marjorie.
My nine lives / by Clio.
p.   cm.
"An Anne Schwartz book."
Summary: Purports to be the journal of a cat recounting all nine of the lives she
has lived and her remarkable effect on history, beginning in Mesopotamia in 3000
B.C. and culminating in Wisconsin in 1995.
ISBN 0-689-81135-7
[1. Cats—Fiction. 2. World history—Fiction. 3. Diaries—Fiction.] I. Title.
PZ7.P932My   1998
[E]—dc21
97-47565

My Nine Lives

by Clio

AN ANNE SCHWARTZ BOOK
Atheneum Books for Young Readers

A note from the Publisher:
One recent morning, we received a large brown envelope in the mail. It contained a tattered old book and the following letter:

Dear Publisher,

I have stumbled upon a remarkable discovery. While searching the house for my cat, Clio, I found what looked like her journal under an old couch. Although Clio is awfully clever, I never knew her talents extended beyond climbing drapes and prying the lids off cheese containers—until now.

Might you be interested in publishing this?

Yours truly,

Mamie Pennyfellow

First Class Mail

JUNE 17
2 PM

USA 32
32 USA
USA 32
USA 20

Atheneum Books for Young Readers
1230 Avenue of the Americas
New York, New York 10020

RUSH!

At first we thought it was a hoax. But after careful examination, the book truly appears to be the journal of a cat who has lived nine different lives in nine different historical times! We decided we couldn't keep this important document a secret. So we've published the highlights for you to read.

Life #1

Mesopotamia
3000 B.C.

me

Alive! I yawn.

I look around.

I am in Mesopotamia, the "land between two rivers." I see fields of wheat and rivers full of fish. I am getting hungry.

At a farm, a man gives me some milk.

At the river, I catch a fish and a crab catches me.

At market, I find a fat crow and some water.

The sun is setting as I climb the temple steps.

On the roof of the temple I lay my feast of fish, crab, crow, a little dipper of milk and a big dipper of water. I look down at my dinner. I look up at the sky. I see groups of stars in the shapes of a fish, a crab, a crow, a big dipper and a little dipper. I give the constellations names! Then I eat.

Life #2 China 1500 B.C.

It is lunchtime at the Ting house, where I live with Mr. Ting and Mrs. Ting and their daughter, Lu. Mrs. Ting rings the lunch bell from the house that wears a hat just like the people do.

Mr. Ting and I are far away in the garden. He cannot hear the bell.

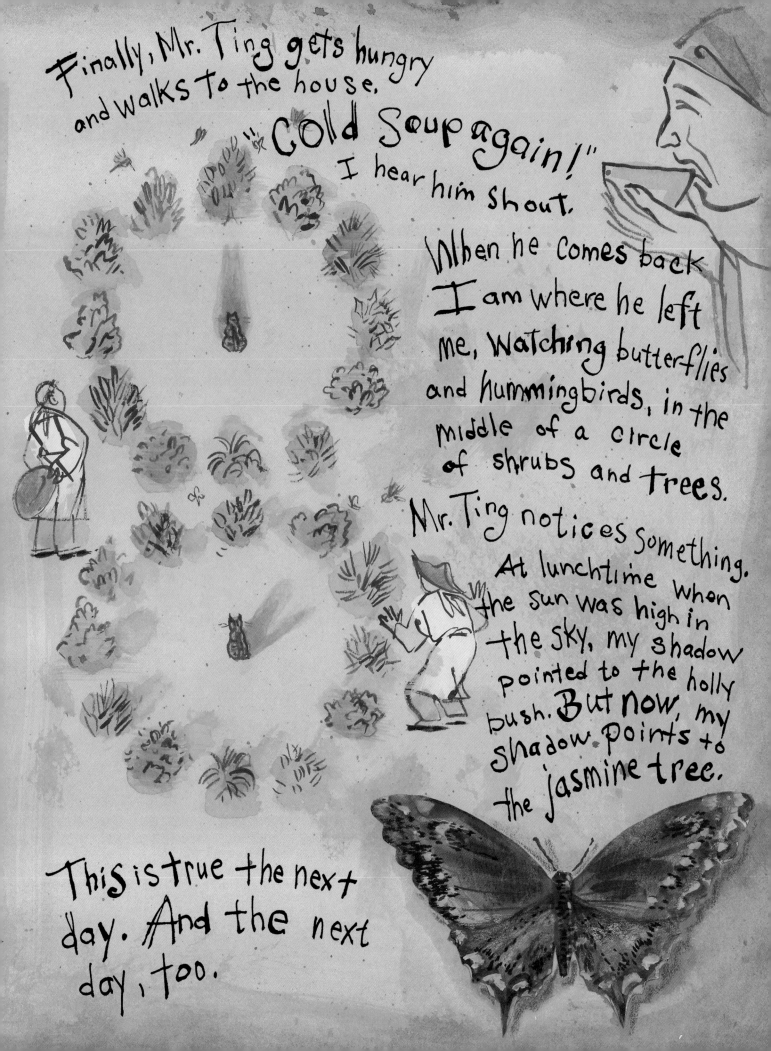

Finally, Mr. Ting gets hungry and walks to the house. "Cold soup again!" I hear him shout.

When he comes back I am where he left me, watching butterflies and hummingbirds, in the middle of a circle of shrubs and trees.

Mr. Ting notices something. At lunchtime when the sun was high in the sky, my shadow pointed to the holly bush. But now, my shadow points to the jasmine tree.

This is true the next day. And the next day, too.

Mr. Ting picks up
his shears.
He clips the holly bush.

He clips the yew tree.
He clips the jasmine,

the willow and

the spruce.

I am a CLOCK! The first one in the world! Now Mr. Ting is never late for lunch, unless it's cloudy or I'm off chasing butterflies...

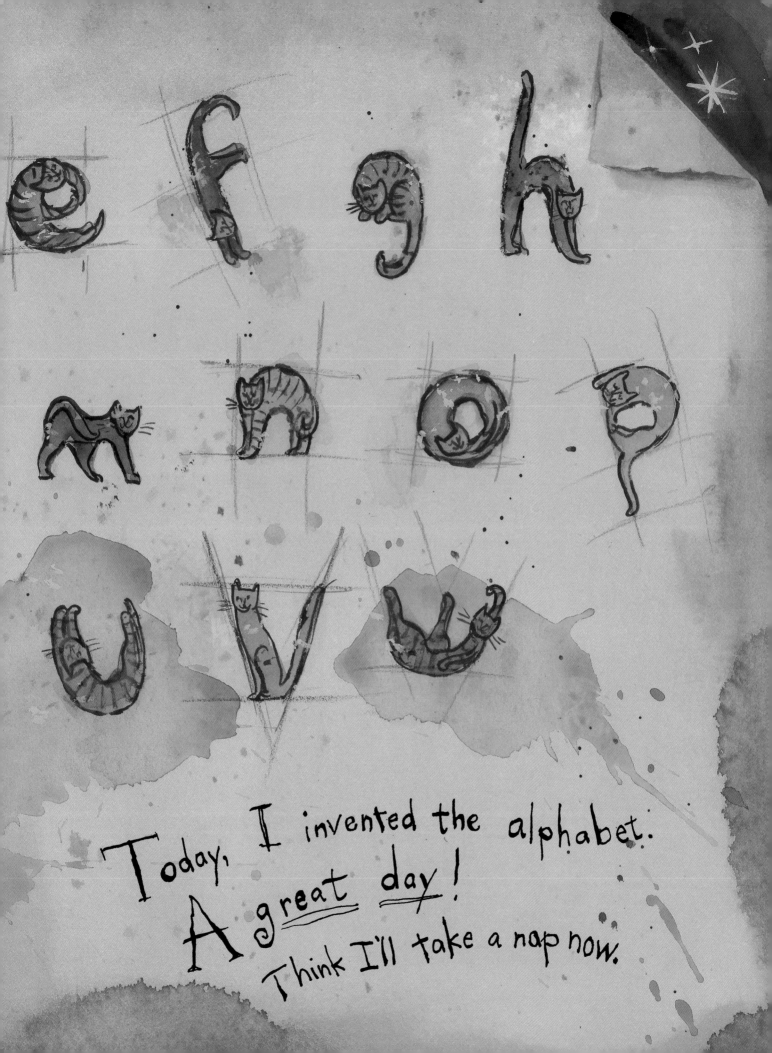

Today, I invented the alphabet.
A great day!
Think I'll take a nap now.

Life #4 At Sea 1000 A.D.

GREENLAND

ICELAND

ATLANTIC OCEAN

Today we set sail from Iceland in rough seas. I'm feeling a little seasick. I'll write more tomorrow.

A new day! I feel much better. I played with some rope. Almost caught a fish. Found some good places to nap.

Captain E.

We've been sailing for awhile now. I'm starting to feel at home. At night I sit in the crow's nest and look for land or other ships or icebergs or whales. With my superior 👁 👁 eyes, I can see in the dark. And, with my excellent ears, I can hear a storm coming from far away. But enough about me...

Hey! Is that a bird?
Think I'll say hello.

Hello, bird.

I pounce.

I grab the mast.
It shudders and shakes.
The bird flies away.

The sail unfurls.
The ship spins.
It sails off...
in the other direction.

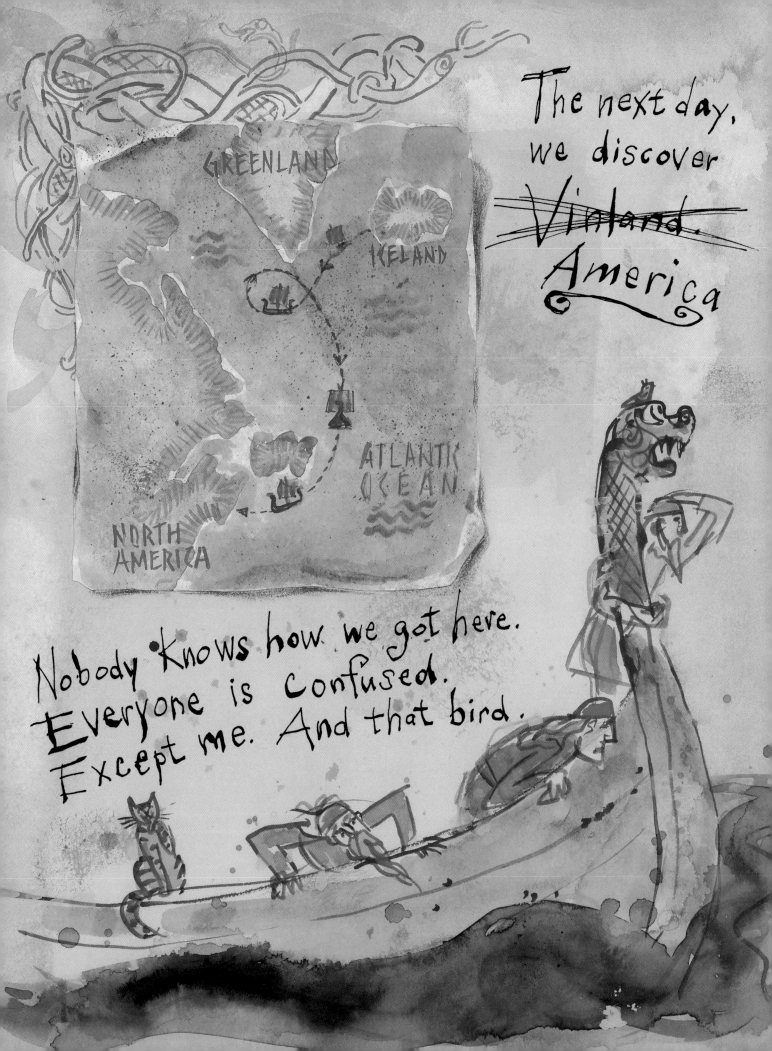

GREENLAND

ICELAND

The next day, we discover ~~Vinland.~~ America

ATLANTIC OCEAN

NORTH AMERICA

Nobody knows how we got here. Everyone is confused. Except me. And that bird.

Terrible times to be feline.

I live in the castle.

King Edward is feared by everyone.

The peasants who till his soil.

The servants who scrub his floors.

Even the Jester.

Even the dog.

And, especially, me.

The King is <u>not</u> fond of Cats.

Only Millie, the cook, likes me.
(I keep the kitchen
floor clean.)

Millie is stirring a stew.
A potato gets loose!
I spear it with my claws.
"Brilliant," says Millie, "I wish
I had a claw tool, too."

Millie does a scientific study.
She finds an old crown lying
around and hammers it into shape.
Millie thinks our invention
looks like a pitchfork so she
names it a "fork."

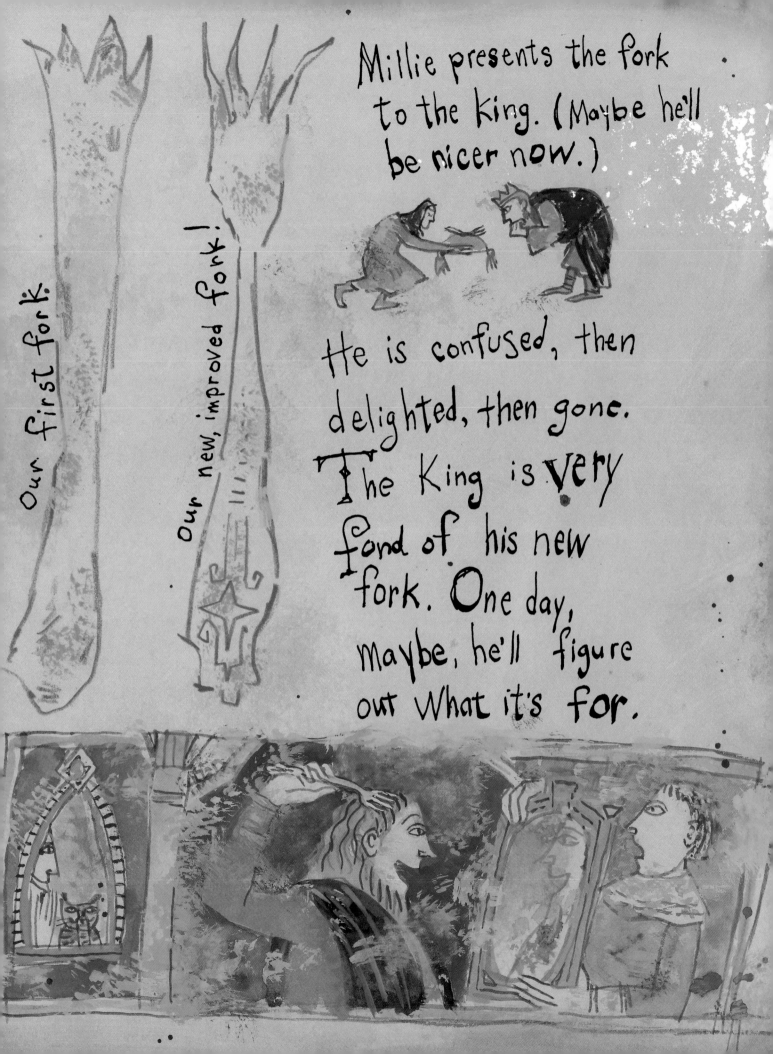

Our first fork.

Our new, improved fork!

Millie presents the fork to the king. (Maybe he'll be nicer now.)

He is confused, then delighted, then gone. The King is very fond of his new fork. One day, maybe, he'll figure out what it's for.

LIFE #6 ~ ITALY ~ 1500

I live with Leonardo, an artist and inventor. I keep the studio free from mice. Leo rewards me with cheese.

I catch a lot of

I eat a lot of

(mozzarella, parmesan, ricotta, fontina, romano)

ITALIA

EUROPA

We sit at the window and
watch birds in flight.
Leo gets an **idea**.
A new invention.
A flying machine!

Leo makes many sketches.

When it is finished,
we travel to the hillside
to test it out.

I am strapped in.
I take flight.

The machine
creaks,
then bends,
then cracks.
The cheese has taken its toll.
Sorry, Leonardo!
The experiment is a flop.
But Oh!
The views!

me

me again

me

Leo likes to paint me because I am good at staying still.

Today, Leo is painting the portrait of a sad lady. I jump on her lap. I purr. She smiles! "Bravo," says Leo. My work is done. Leo paints a masterpiece.

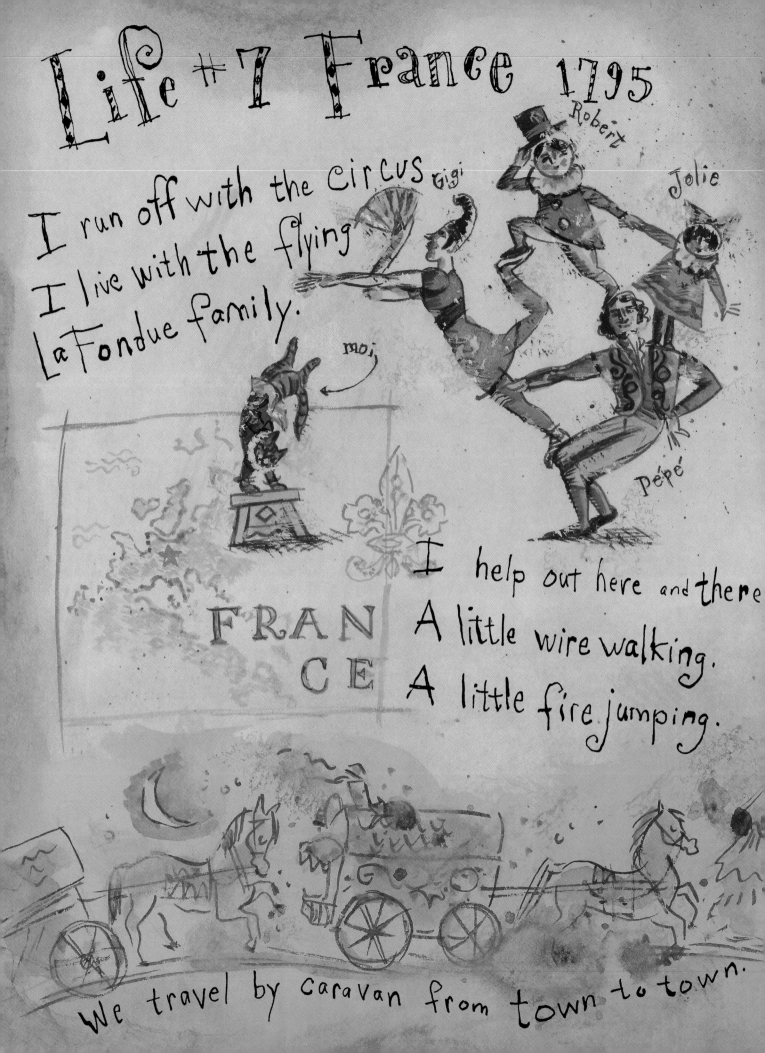

Life #7 France 1795

I run off with the CIRCUS.
I live with the flying
LaFondue family.

Gigi
Robert
Jolie
moi
Pépé

I help out here and there
A little wire walking.
A little fire jumping.

FRAN
CE

We travel by caravan from town to town.

We set up in Paris. It is 20 degrees. Pépé has caught cold and can't go on. He asks me to take his place in the trapeze act. "I'd like to," I say. "But..." Too late. He is gone. Doesn't he know that cats don't have opposable thumbs for grasping objects like people do?

I find myself on a platform, forty feet up.

BILLET
13 JUN TO 1384

There's no turning back now.
one, two, three...I reach for
the trapeze......OOOOOOoohhh
NOOOOOOOOoooooo.....

Life #8 New Orleans 1913

Have you heard Razz and his band? They're the hippest group around. They've got that ultimate, sky-high, shimmy, shimmy, toe-tickling Sound.

Yours truly Razz

But it wasn't always So. Oh no, no, no, no, no, no, _no!_

Life #9

Wisconsin
U.S.A.
1995

Behind bars!
And for NO good reason!
I was simply taking a nap in a
flower garden and I wake up
in jail !!!

CITY POUND

"But not for long.
Mamie Pennyfellow rescues me and brings me home to her nice yellow house. ➤

Say "CHEESE" you're in... WISCONSIN.

It's a paradise! Soft rugs, plump pillows. A fireplace!

And in the yard, a catnip patch!

When Mamie knits, she lets me play with the yarn.

Actual yarn!

Remy has come to live with us (I think Mamie got him out of jail, too). At first, we fight over the easy chair...

though soon we are the <u>best</u> of friends.

Remy brings me a fat swiss cheese, but, for some reason, today I crave Sardines...

Leo's first flea.

Clio & Remy
are pleased
to announce
the birth of
4 daughters
and
5 Sons!

Millie's first
hairball.

What luck! Nine new lives.
There's so much to do.
So much to look forward to!

Mona 4 oz.

Leif
4.1 oz.

Millie 3.5 oz.

Remy, Jr.
3.8 oz.

Leo 4.7 oz.

Pépe 4.4 oz.

Romano 5 oz.

Fontina
4.3 oz.

Ricotta
3.9 oz.

We, the publishers, hope you have enjoyed Clio's journal.

But perhaps you are wondering, "Could this all be true?" We wondered ourselves. So we have consulted a team of historians, veterinarians, cartographers, chemists, and handwriting experts. Here is what we found out.

Life #1 Mesopotamia

Most historians agree that the Sumerians of Mesopotamia were the first to locate and name the constellations. Also, the pictures are similar in style to ancient artifacts found in that part of the world.

Life #2 China

There is evidence that an early form of the sundial was first developed in China around this time. (It was called a "gnomon" and was simply a stick that cast a shadow.) But obviously Arabic numerals were not used. There are also experts who believe that Egypt was the birthplace of the first time-telling device.

Life #3 Rome

Experts agree that our alphabet is a modern version of the Roman alphabet. But the original Roman alphabet was believed to have had only twenty-one letters. Our scientists have revealed that a stain (possibly tomato sauce) was concealing the letters j, u, v, y, and z for many years until it faded or was washed away, maybe after exposure to water.

Life #4 At Sea

Captain E. is probably Leif Eriksson, the Viking explorer who first set foot in North America. (The Vikings called it Vinland.) It was generally believed that trade winds blew his ship off course, but Clio's account seems plausible. Our cryptologist has discovered some runes (Viking letters) hidden in the pictures but hasn't had time to decipher them. The Viking alphabet is printed below if you'd like to try yourself.

f   u   th a   r   k   h   n   i   a   s   t   b   m   l   r

ᚠ   ᚢ   ᚦ   ᚨ   ᚱ   ᚲ   ᚺ   ᚾ   ᛁ   ᛏ   ᛊ   ᛏ   ᛒ   ᛗ   ᛚ   ᛦ

Life #5 England

Crude versions of the modern fork have been unearthed by archaeologists digging in Turkey. These tools are estimated to have been made from 6,000 to 3,000 B.C. But there is no further evidence of forks until 1307 when a document listing the possessions of Edward I mentions seven forks, one made of gold.

Life #6 Italy
Leonardo is clearly Leonardo da Vinci, the famed painter and inventor who lived during the time known as the Renaissance. The sketches in Clio's journal are quite similar to those in da Vinci's own sketchbooks. Chemists have determined that the various drips and smudges on the pages are indeed oil paint. Although da Vinci is believed to be a genius whose ideas were far ahead of his time, he never did make a successful flying machine. And art experts have always considered the source of Mona Lisa's smile one of the great mysteries of all time. Perhaps the mystery has been solved.

Life #7 France
The word *parachute* is French. (*Para* is from parasol and *chute* means fall.) Some scholars have produced evidence that Chinese acrobats as early as 1306 used parachute-like devices. But the modern parachute was first used successfully by a French man named André-Jacques Garnerin in 1797. In 1802 Garnerin patented his parachute. It is possible that Garnerin was in the crowd at the circus that day and saw Clio's spectacular landing.

Life #8 New Orleans, United States
Music scholars agree that New Orleans was the birthplace of jazz. Nobody can quite agree how jazz got its name, though some say in 1913 there was a Dixieland group called Razz's band, and somehow or another it was changed to "Jazz band."

Life #9 Wisconsin, United States
An expert at the post office verified that the package containing Clio's journal was indeed mailed from Wisconsin. An official at the city pound recorded the adoption of one brown tabby cat, female, age 8 months by one Mamie Pennyfellow on July 12, 1995. The catnip is of a variety that grows in the Midwest. A faint odor of cheddar cheese was noted by all.

Some additional notes:
*Most historians believe that paper (and therefore journals) did not exist until
  it was invented in Egypt in the first century.
*There is no explanation as to why the journal is written entirely in English,
  instead of languages appropriate to the particular times and places.
*Most veterinarians say that cats are not capable of writing or even holding a
  pen.
*It has been pointed out that if the alphabet wasn't invented until Life #3, then
  how were lives #1 and #2 written?
*The paper airplane in Life #6 is remarkably similar to the Super-Sonic
  Transport.
*The squashed bug on page three of Life #5 is from 1996.